Albert
the
confused
manatee

Written and Illustrated by
Christopher Straub

First Edition
Design and layout: Christopher Straub
Straub, Christopher
Albert the Confused Manatee
ISBN-13: 978-0-692-25821-7
Printed in China

www.christopherstraub.com
www.confusedmanatee.com

To mom.

Albert is a bit confused.

He doesn't know what kind of animal he is.

Albert has lots of friends in the ocean that can help him figure it out.

Let's go!

"Am I an octopus?" Albert asks his slippery friend.

"No, silly, you're a manatee! Sure, we both live in the ocean but I have eight arms."

"You're right." Albert says. "Thank you so much!"

Albert continues on his journey.

"Am I a shark?" Albert asks his sharp-toothed friend.

"No, silly, you're a manatee! Sure, we both use our tails to swim but I eat meat."

"OH MY...I see!" Albert says.
"Thank you."

Albert quickly swims away.

"Am I a seahorse?" Albert asks his colorful friend.

"No, silly, you're a manatee! Sure, we both live among the seaweed but I'm WAY smaller than you."

"Oh yeah!" Albert says. "Thank you!"

So he keeps swimming.

"Am I an orca?" Albert asks his mighty friend.

"No, silly, you're a manatee! Sure, we both breathe air but I have a dorsal fin on my back."

"I see that now." Albert says.
"Thank you so much!"

Albert continues on his journey.

"Am I a seal?" Albert asks his playful friend.

"No, silly, you're a manatee! Sure, we both have flippers but our tails look different."

"Oh, yeah!" Albert says. "Thank you!"

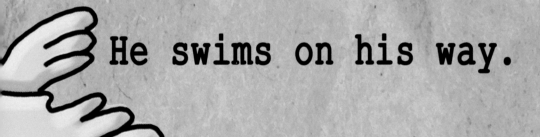 He swims on his way.

"Am I a narwhal?" Albert asks his strange-looking friend.

"No, silly, you're a manatee! Sure, we are both grey but I have a horn on my head."

"Oh yeah, I see." Albert says.
"Thank you!"

Albert continues on his journey.

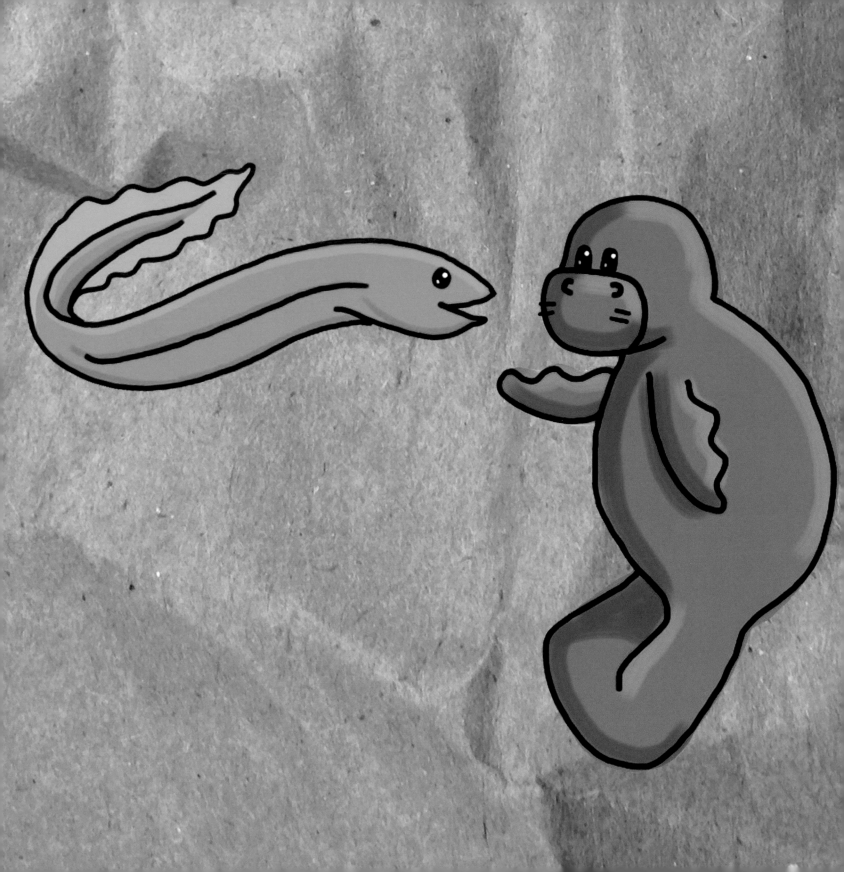

"Am I an eel?" Albert asks his slimy friend.

"No, silly, you're a manatee! Sure, we both live underwater but I'm a fish and you're a mammal."

"That's right!" Albert says. "Thank you!"

Albert continues on his way.

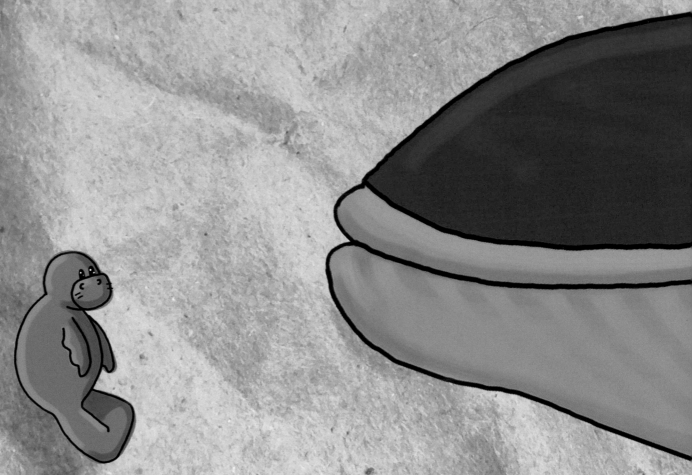

"Am I a blue whale?" Albert asks his giant friend.

"No, silly, you're a manatee! Sure, we are both slow swimmers but I'm WAY bigger than you."

"Oh, WOW, you ARE really big!"
Albert says. "Thank you!"

Albert keeps swimming.

"Am I a clownfish?" Albert asks his tiny friend.

"No, silly, you're a manatee! Sure, we both live in shallow water but I have striped, scaly skin."

"I see that now." Albert says. "Thank you so much!"

So he continues on his way.

"Am I an alligator?" Albert asks his scaly friend.

"No, silly, you're a manatee! Sure, we both spend the day relaxing but I can go on land."

"Of course." Albert says. "Thank you!"

Albert continues on his journey.

"Am I a sea turtle?" Albert asks his green friend.

"No, silly, you're a manatee! Sure, we both swim long distances but I have a hard shell on my back."

"Oh yeah!" Albert says. "Thank you!"

So he swims on his way.

"Am I a starfish?" Albert asks his pointy friend.

"No silly, you're a manatee! Sure, we both dig in the sand but I breathe underwater and you breathe air."

"Oh yeah." Albert says. "Thank you for your help."

Albert continues swimming.

"Am I a pufferfish?" Albert asks his spiny friend.

"No, silly, you're a manatee! Sure, we don't like to be frightened but I have sharp spikes."

"Oh yeah, I see." Albert says. "Thank you!"

Albert continues on his journey.

"Am I a walrus?" Albert asks his brawny friend.

"No, silly, you're a manatee! Sure, we both have thick skin but I have long tusks."

"That's what those are!" Albert says. "Thank you!"

Albert continues to wander.

Albert has enjoyed learning about his friends but he still hasn't met any animals exactly like him.

Suddenly, Albert sees one more
friend far off in the distance...

"Am I a manatee?" Albert asks the gentle manatee.

"Yes, of course you are! We're both grey, have oval-shaped tails and eat seaweed. We ARE the same animal! We're both manatees!"

Albert is so excited. "I AM A MANATEE and I'm happy to meet you! Thank you so much for helping me!"

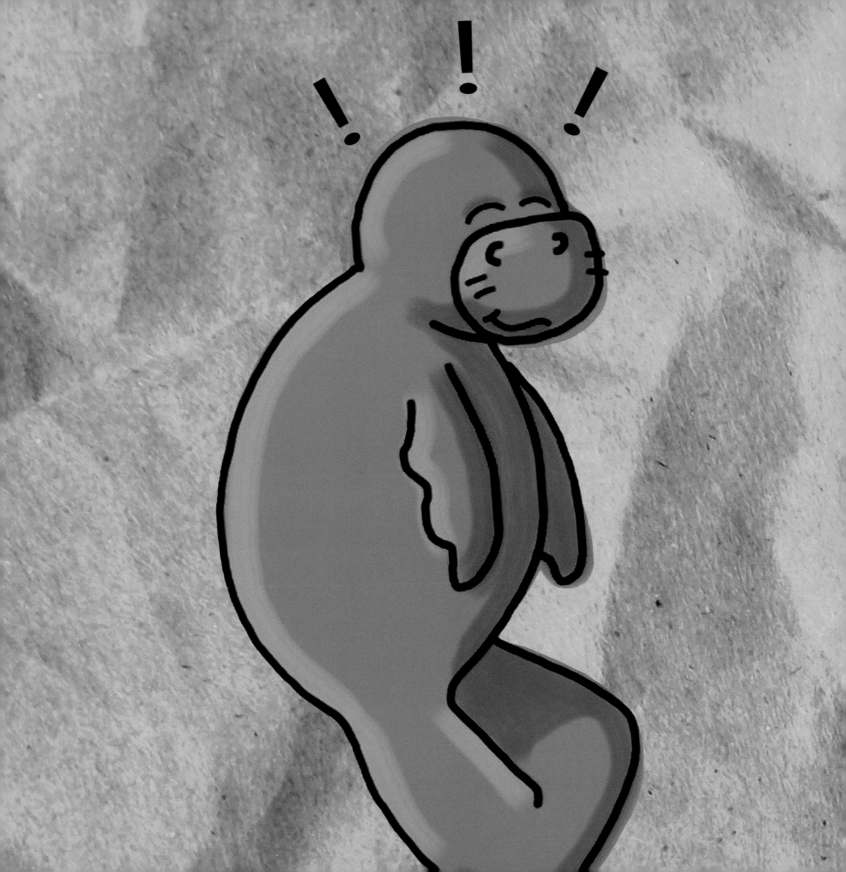

His journey taught him that even though he is different from the other animals he also has a lot in common with them.

Albert is no longer a confused manatee.

About the Author and Illustrator

Christopher Straub is an artist and fashion designer who lives in Shakopee, Minnesota. He's best known for being featured on season 6 of the reality competition series *Project Runway*. His passions are not limited to fashion, however, and include all forms of design.

Since childhood, Straub has had a fascination with manatees and that's what inspired him to write this book. *Albert the Confused Manatee* is his first release as an author… and hopefully not his last.

For more information:

www.ConfusedManatee.com
www.ChristopherStraub.com